Frederick T. Mott

Benscliff Ballads and Other Poems

Frederick T. Mott

Benscliff Ballads and Other Poems

ISBN/EAN: 9783744777186

Printed in Europe, USA, Canada, Australia, Japan

Cover: Foto ©Andreas Hilbeck / pixelio.de

More available books at **www.hansebooks.com**

The Benscliff Ballads

AND OTHER POEMS

BY

F. T. MOTT, F.R.G.S.

AUTHOR OF

'CORONA,' 'KING EDDA'S PARABLES,' ETC.

A BOOK FOR SUMMER HOLIDAYS

GAY AND BIRD

22 BEDFORD STREET, STRAND

LONDON

1899

PREFACE

WE were ten
Middle-aged men,
Slaves of the ledger, the desk, and the pen.

Providence having selected us from the most diverse creeds and parties, and baptized us into the Faith of Friendship, we met at intervals for high talk, under the motto 'Firm heart, free tongue'; and spent on rare occasions a Midsummer Day's Dream together among the hills and woods of Charnwood Forest. Benscliff was our favourite rendezvous.

CONTENTS

CONTENTS

𝔒biter 𝔠antata, *continued*—

𝔐emorials—

NOTE.—Some of the pieces in this volume have been already published, but are here collected.

The Benscliff Ballads

THE TROPIC SUMMER, 1868

WELCOME to my tent, old comrades ! in this burning
    month of June ;
Though the hills are parched and thirsty, and the
    brooks all out of tune,
And the pastures of the valley changed from green
    to whity-brown,
Better frizzle on the hillside than sit roasting in
    the town.

Leave your squabbles at the Castle, let the big-wigs
    fight it out—
Who'll care to-morrow if the battle end in victory
    or rout ?
Leave your waterpipes and discounts, shares won't
    rise in such a sun,
Leave your parchments, Fate will settle all things
    when our deeds are done.

Schools, thank Heaven, don't work in summer !—
　　lock the door and come away ;
Preaching's over, now let's practise, making jovial
　　holiday.
Here's the wine and here the cherries, here our
　　cup of silver bright ;
'Speak the truth and shame the Devil,' and let
　　victory crown the right !

Sitting in the tent's cool shadow, see, the hills are
　　all ablaze
With the fierce and fatal splendour of these golden
　　summer days.
Ruined ! like some fool of fortune, by the glad and
　　prosperous years,
Vainly sighing for a sorrow to enrich his soul with
　　tears !

Ruined with the wealth of sunlight ! Corn and
　　pasture, herb and flower,
Juiceless, lifeless, parched and withered, by a month
　　without a shower !

We have done great things in science—chained the
    lightning, ploughed the main,
Yet our harvest dies around us, lacking but a little
    rain !

Wisdom grows, but ah, how slowly! measured by
    our narrow gaze :
Angel-pulses mark the time off, not in moments,
    but in days ;
While the May-fly thinks at sunset, 'I have lived
    through love and strife,
Changing scenes of joy and trouble, what a long
    and varied life !'

So when Science fills this gap up, doing what is
    now undone,
It shall seem but one more milestone in the circuit
    of the sun.
Age and learning, time and distance, bearing
    Death's broad-arrow mark,
In the glare of the Eternal, die like colours in the
    dark.

There ! Philosophy's refreshing when the heat is
on the hill,
But the deep wood close behind us, moist and
green, is cooler still,—
Cooler than the keenest logic, sweeter than the
happiest thought,
Pleasanter than wine or wisdom in this soul-
exhausting drought.

Here are mosses, ferns, and clambering woodbines,
and in broad green flakes,
Shimmering in the shady wood-light, stand the
curled and stately brakes ;
Here are crags all lichen-crusted, cushioned with
the mountain grass,—
Let us sit and fan the flies off, while the drowsy
moments pass,

Under boughs of pine and chestnut, broad-leaved
sycamore and beech,
Mingling with the golden silence, intervals of
silver speech ;

Till the woods grow dim and ghostly, and the
  night comes whispering down—
Then for home, and lights, and supper, and the
  comforts of the town!

THE CHRISTENING OF THE CUP

A RUSH, a whirl upon the wings of steam,
　　And then a glad heart-greeting;
Smiles and hand-claspings warm, such as beseem
　　Old friends at each new meeting;
Then through the hot and dusty town, away
To the green pillars of the western day.

Fair hills of Charnwood! loveliest in the light
　　Of blue exultant morning,
Grandest when falls the curtain of the night
　　With red and stormful warning;
Up to thy crags we lead our worshipping feet,
And with unspoken praise God's mountain wonders
　　meet.

Through glades and gleaming woods, past aisles
　　of elm,
　　Tall shafts of quivering willow,

6

Banks crowned with plumy fern, like Oberon's helm
　　Hung o'er Titania's pillow;
Under deep arches of grim, sinewy oak,
Where the great light-flood into ripples broke;

　By village homes rose-garlanded, and built
　　For warmth, and use, and beauty
　Of the rich native rock, whose builders felt
　　The weight of a high duty,
And gave, to enrich God's earth for all mankind,
Their wealth of gold, and rarer wealth of mind;

　Far past the grey old church, our cheery steeds
　　The rough slope bravely breasting,
　We passed, where, high above the cultured meads,
　　Torn crags the summit cresting,
A ferny ridge, like some green mamelon steep
Of Nature's fortress, guards her loftier keep.

　There next, ascending slow by grassy ways
　　Through a green wilderness winding,
　We stood, eight human brothers, in the blaze
　　Of the slant sunshine, binding
With chains of happy memories heart to heart,
Anchors of friendship which no gales shall part.

Where once the Bale-fire burned, we standing
   round
   A fair-wrought silver chalice
Brimmed with bright bubbling wine, from that old
   mound,
   Called on the hills and valleys
To witness how, in the rich draught there lay
A pledge of endless brotherhood, sealed that day.

So was our sacred Cup right nobly born
   In the clear evening hour,
Midst rock and breeze, fit symbols to adorn
   Friendship's unguarded tower!
Firm heart!   Free tongue! these be our watch-
   words bold,
Keen glittering silver, lined with changeless gold.

From the bright hilltop, when our rites were done,
   Down broad green slopes descending
We passed, and saw the slowly dropping sun
   A mellower beauty lending
To ivy-fretted walls, and pale-eyed flowers
That peep and twinkle out of forest bowers;

Past the broad Outwoods, past the Great Buck
    Hill,
  Round by the famed Nan-pantan,
O'er whose grey forehead Hesperus rose, to fill
    With light his glimmering lantern,
So to the flowery alleys and green shades
Of Longcliffe, winding far among its mazy glades;

  Till night, with all her starry watch, drew down
    The faded sky, and closing
  The forest gates with darkness, to their town
    Warned back the wanderers: losing
Only the vision, not the memory, still
We seemed to tread the woodpath and the hill.

  And then once more the rush of steam.   Farewell!
    Good night, brave friends and brothers!
  A longer night is coming; none may tell
    Who first shall leave the others!
But the great Love in whose wide arms we lie
Will guard His own.   It is no loss to die.

THE ULVERSCROFT VALLEY

MIDSUMMER blazed on the forest,
  All fragrant with roses and hay ;
The hills and the silent woodlands
  Lay asleep in the broad noonday.

Oh for the light and the stillness !
  We dwellers in Radical towns,
Are we wiser, among our chimneys,
  Than the calm-eyed country clowns ?

They learn one lesson from Nature,
  We learn another from Art ;
Both read in the Book of Beauty,
  And each sees only a part.

But we who are lovers of all things,
  The new and the ancient ways,
Would round our souls to the universe
  With large and equal gaze.

So we plunged in the heart of the forest,
    Where the larch and the Norway pine
With the elms and the oaks of England
    Their wild boughs intertwine;

Where the lake lay bright in the sunshine,
    With scarcely a ripple to show
How the swans in the burnished mirror
    Swam double, above and below.

The elder-flower and the foxglove,
    By the woods and the grassy leas,
Made a splendour of ermine and purple
    Out-glorying the Tuilleries.

And a calm, disdainful echo
    Came back from oak and fir,
To the song of our Gallic hero—
    'La gloire de l'Empereur!'

For a sculptor may mould the surface,
    But a tree grows from the heart;
And what is the pomp of empire
    But the vulgarest trick of art?

Far in the Ulverscroft valley,
   Under the Benscliff woods,
A symbol of British freedom,
   A little estate of eight roods

Lies alone among lordly neighbours,
   Broad acres where titled boys
Sport with the fox and the pheasant,
   As a child with its wooden toys.

Here we pitched our tent on the greensward,
   Here friendship's feast was spread,
And we drank to the Past and the Future—
   'Our Club, the living and dead !

'Our Cup and its sacred memories !'
   For the name and the spirit of him
Who has left our genial circle,
   Still live on its silver brim.

And we know that a day is coming
   When our part in the world shall be
Like his, a thought and a vision,
   A name and a memory.

O friends, is it hard to convince us
    That the true and the real are unseen?
Have we not learned to measure
    What life and its forces mean?

By the spirit of Love, which is mightiest,
    By a noble trust in the good,
Unmoved through all visible changes,
    We stand where our fathers stood.

And ever the sway of the hero,
    And the strength of the poet's word,
Grows when the mighty is fallen,
    And the song is no more heard.

    .   .   .   .   .

Soon from that sun-lighted garden
    We passed, through a woodland gate,
Into the shades of the forest,
    Where the flowers seem to listen and wait;

Into the regions of silence,
    Unbroken by bird or stream,
Where the fern stands in motionless armies,
    And the great trees whisper and dream.

Climbing by cliff and through bracken,
  We stood on the craggy brow,
And reckoned the strange, wild ages
  Which moulded the marvellous Now ;

The myriads of summers and winters,
  The fires and the frosts and the floods,
Which have built up the bones of this planet,
  And decked it with daisy-buds.

Then from that rock-built temple
  With loitering feet we pass,
Down through the shadowy woodlands
  To our tent on the new-mown grass,

Where the fragrant tea and the roses,
  The fruit and the cake and the tongue,
Rekindled the fainting fires
  In flagging brain and lung.

Like giants refreshed, some reclining
  Fed their eyes on the prospect fair,
While the clang of the classic discus
  Rang sharp in the evening air.

And worthy of Phœbus Apollo
    Was the welcome of light and song
Which rose from the hills of old Charnwood
    To those who had loved them long ;

From Timberwood, Birchtree, and Hammercliff,
    Crowned with a glory of green ;
From the beautiful Ulverscroft valley
    Like a leafy lake between ;

From Chitterman, veiled in oak-wreaths,
    From Markfield's rocky brows,
The joy of that forest welcome
    In a flush of beauty rose.

For Nature greets her children
    With a mother's glad caress,
And they whom she loves shall enter
    The kingdom of happiness.

Now the broad wings of the sunset,
    With plumage of purple and gold,
Gather the hills and the woodlands
    Under their mystic fold.

And the tender moon unnoticed
  Sails up the eastern sky,
Copying with delicate pencil
  The shadows before they die.

And we on the skirts of the twilight
  Follow the darkness home,
While the last farewells of Nature
  Drop from her starry dome.

It was a day as soft and warm and balmy
  As ever breathed upon our blusterous Isle;
No Indian sky to jungles damp and palmy
    E'er deigned so sweet a smile.

And we were eight—eight fellows brisk and jolly,
  Bound for the hills, and primed with boyish glee
To catch bright laughter from the face of folly,
    And save a doctor's fee.

Eight fellows, all philosophers in earnest,
  Spending in sport the beauty of one day!
Think twice, O solemn critic, ere thou turnest
    Thy scornful eyes away.

First crack this nut :—Th' Omnipotent made all
    things—
  Wisdom and folly, nettles, flowers, and food;
And this stands sure, whatever we may call things,
    He made them all for good.

B

In that brave faith, so beautiful and cheery,
  We met the sunshine with a thankful joy,
Voting dull logic out of place, and dreary
    As syntax to a boy.

By soft Arcadian brooks we sang old ditties,
  And plucked the blackberries and cracked the
    jokes,
And wondered whether life in crowded cities
    Were not a monstrous hoax.

For all the birds and all the shining grasses,
  The glens and leafy dingles, seemed to say
With simple tongues—'What! is it *man* who passes
    Blind eyed the golden day?

· We have heard legends of this wondrous creature,
  So bright, so beautiful, so formed to rule;
We had not dreamed that perfect shape and feature
    Might clothe a fool!'

Perhaps we had no answer to this query;
  Perhaps we thought, and didn't care to speak;
No matter, even poetic legs grow weary,
    And thirsty souls are weak.

As once, 'tis said, parched Israel rose and hurried
  To that new rock-stream in the fiery plain,
So rose our hearts exultant, when we buried
    Our lips in cool champagne.

And then a mile or two between tall hedges,
  Hung thick with clustering berries black and red,
And lo ! we stood upon the slaty ledges
    Of Beacon's royal head.

Fair queen of hills ! though half a million winters
  Have chipped thy diadem and scarred thy brow,
We love thee better decked in all thy splinters
    And painted by the plough.

The summer clouds drop kindly shadows o'er thee,
  The bending woodlands worship at thy feet,
And eager winds rush headlong to adore thee
    With kisses fresh and sweet.

O stand for ever, beautiful and lonely !
  And grant us all, with city cares oppressed,
This annual gift of grace—for one day only
    To dream upon thy breast !

Sed omnia mutant—(extract made to order)
     The sky was changing, *il fallut que nous*
Should go to tea, for on the vale's green border
     Our banquet lay in view.

Philosophy does not include starvation ;
     Mensa sub Jove, ham *cum* pigeon-pie ;
Was never seen a welcomer collation
     Beneath a summer sky !

So, all being over, and the carriage ready,
     We left the hills, grey in the waning light,
And as the woods closed round us, felt already
     The cool wings of the Night.

Profound and holy ! mother of to-morrow,
     And sweet consoler of the wearied Day ;
Night, whose arge pity hideth sin and sorrow
     Beneath her sheltering sway !

Mirth for the sunshine, laughter for the morning,
     But the pure stars bring silence, lovelier still ;
Folly stands awestruck, and a voiceless warning
     Commands the vagrant will.

So let us part, old friends, this night and ever,
  Not sad but earnest, looking towards the day
When every noble deed and brave endeavour
  Shall have its wreath of bay.

BIRSTAL HILL

Once more, old friends, to prove this world an Eden,
    And Man its noblest plant,
That Paradise is not confined to Sweden,[1]
    Nor happiness to Cant—
We'll to the hills, where Nature keeps her Sabbath
  With merry bird, gay flower, and dancing brook
Seven days a week, and needs no priestly sanction,
    No altar and no book.

Here gleams the pool, there the green wood encloses
    Farmstead and sunny croft ;
The peaceful village in its vale reposes,
    The grey crags tower aloft.
We climb the heights, and in the hazy distance
  Behold that mightiest work of unfledged art,
The human town, that beats in Nature's bosom
    Like a strong central heart.

---

[1] It is said to have been proved that the Garden of Eden was
in Scandinavia.

The lowliest things soar soonest to perfection,
   The dewdrop and the flower;
Man, gathering force through æons of selection,
   Still waits the crowning hour.
Already in his soul the coming Beauty
  Pours out her music from the spheres above,
The martyr and the patriot die for duty,
   And friendship blooms in love.

But who shall dream what greatness lies before him?
   Child of the innocent Earth,
The glory of the future brooding o'er him
   Shines dimly round his birth.
A thousand centuries, perhaps no more, have
     laboured
  To rear for Heaven this royal son of Time;
Millions shall make him strong and wise and holy,
   And lead him to his prime.

So, my brave comrades, friends through sixteen
     summers,
   As ministers of Hope,
We'll guard the joy of life against all comers,
   From Calvin to the Pope.

We 'll quaff old port beside the Benscliff larches,
  With song and joke the forest echoes fill,
Then brim with liquid gold our silver goblet,
    And drink to Birstal Hill !

May never blight or mildew, grub or canker,
    Its rosy bowers despoil ;
Let Strength meet Beauty there, and Love cast
      anchor
    Deep in its fruitful soil ;
And till grey age shall teach their feet to falter,
  And hang death's veil before their fading eyes,
May friendship, such as ours, which cannot alter,
    Be their best prize !

THE DAUGHTER OF THE MAYOR

I

A WEALTHY Borough, proud to know
    Its ancient charter bore
Sign-manual of the grand old Duke
    Who ruled in days of yore
Back from these noisy modern times
    Four hundred years and more,

Summons yet once again its men
    Of wisdom, wealth, and skill,
Its Aldermen and Councillors,
    To speak their sovereign will,
And choose what worthiest citizen
    Their civic throne may fill.

There meet grey beards and tawny locks,
    The burly and the slim,

Bold touters for the public breath,
   Old veterans grave and grim,
With many an honest prejudice
   And many a hopeless whim.

Stands one apart, a lithe, pale man,
   Black-bearded and broad-browed,
Some unknown strain of gentler blood
   Uplifts him from the crowd;
And when his name is whispered low,
   All tongues consent aloud.

A manful heart, a ready hand,
   A spirit quick and bold,
He grasps the rudder of command
   With firm and vigorous hold,
While yet his heart is on the hills
   With crags and forests old.

And when he leaves the judgment-seat,
   The river's reedy brim,
The ferny wood, the lichened rock,
   Have dearer charms for him

Than palace, park, or painted hall,
  Or studious chamber dim.

And ever with him goes his child,
  A flower of beauty rare,
Her eyes warm jewels set in jet,
  A sable cloud her hair;
And well the forest children know
  The daughter of the Mayor,

For yearly, in the hawthorn-time,
  Before the hay goes down,
To keep her summer festival
  She leaves the dusky town,
And makes her dwelling on the hills
  Until the fern be brown.

There in the sunny summer days,
  Her soul in some quaint book,
By craggy uplands wild and bare,
  Green glen or flowery nook,
She saunters slow, or sits alone
  Beside some forest brook.

Not morbid with ignoble dreams,
    Not 'melancholy mad,'
But pondering problems of the soul—
Why toil should win so poor a dole,
    And life should be so sad—
She hears Earth's calm reply, and learns
    To worship and be glad ;

To know the secret of true joy,
    To feel all human need,
To lavish with unstinted love
    The helpful word and deed,
Or drop along the paths of life
    Good thoughts like fruitful seed.

Sweet days of calm, unconscious growth,
    Like all things strong and wild !
Sweet sunset hours that bless each day
    The father and the child
With happy greeting !   Hours of love
    And duty reconciled.

II

To Nature's shrine, all leaf-inlaid,
  Where whispering streamlets run,
On a May morning comes her priest
  To worship in the sun,
And from the bursting clover-buds
  To learn how heaven is won.

He kneels upon the shining grass
  Beside a purple flower,
Nor dreams what weight of fortune hangs
  Upon that fateful hour,
What wandering angel steals unheard
  Into his woodland bower.

Like morning glory on the hills,
  Like moonlight on the plain,
Or splendour of a sudden thought
  Upon a labouring brain,
The vision floods his lifted eyes
  Like rush of summer rain.

O mysteries of love, behind
    Earth's tinted veil that lie!
O Hand of God, that holds supreme
    The helm of destiny!
We know not, see not, dream not, though
    The crown of life be nigh.

III

Summer and winter, and again
    The land in beauty lay.
At Nature's shrine two hearts knelt down
    Among the flowers of May,
And they were crowned!   Earth never knew
    A lovelier marriage-day.

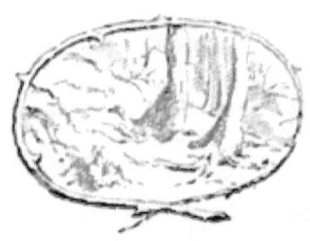

WHAT COULD IT BE?

High on the tops of the mountains of Charnwood,
  Thousands of feet from the depths of the sea,
Gathered a company stalwart and beautiful,
  Just the *élite* of this land of the free.

The Smiths and the Joneses, the Browns and the
      Robinsons,
  Names if not famous in history's pages,
'Tis because history always is written
  By ignorant cads who pretend to be sages !

There in the arms of the Benscliff plantations,
  Full in the blaze of the afternoon sun,
Sat that brave company laughing and rollicking,
  Eating and drinking and splitting with fun.

What is the beauty of evening or morning,
  What is the splendour of tropical skies,
To the rousing delight of a day in the forest,
  With thousands of flowers and millions of flies !

31

Talk about Italy, Norway, or Switzerland !
  Look at those hills and that valley between—
Earth has no ruin to vie with old Ulverscroft,
  Woods so umbrageous or meadows so green !

Well may the pride and the fashion of Leicestershire
  Fly to these scenes for their holiday sprees,
Here they may bask in the freshness of Nature,
  No germs in the water, no blacks on the trees.

Life is worth living and laughter enjoyable
  Here, with the lizard, the frog, and the snake ;
To have beetles all over them, earwigs and cock-
    chafers,
  Well may the wealthy their mansions forsake !

This was the secret, no doubt, of that company's
  Jovial encampment that day on the grass.
Merry and frolicsome, happy as butterflies,
  How should they guess what was coming to pass ?

Nature is fair, but she's often deceitful,
  So is a woman—and so is a man.
Samson was gulled by the faithless young Délilah,
  So were the lions by faithful old Dan.

Was it that thunder growled fierce in the distance ?
Was it that spiders were found in the tea ?
A bear in the forest ? a comet uncanny ?
Something was coming ! but what could it be ?

They listened, they wondered, they searched the
plantations,
They looked up the chimney, they peeped in the
well.
What was this terrible thing that was coming,
And where would it come from ? Could nobody
tell ?

The ladies turned pale, they were trembling with
terror ;
The men, like bold heroes, to comfort them strove,
But horror infected them—something was
coming !
When somebody cried—'It's *to-morrow*, by Jove !'

A PARTY went out on a midsummer day,
A party of idlers bent on play.
Who would work when the sun was so hot
That he frizzled the bacon and boiled the pot?
There was Alderman Spinner and little boy Jack,
And old Father Beeswax and Sydney the black,
And Susie and Polly and brave Parson Hopps,
And Willie and Annie, two Kates, and our Pops.
But of all that fine dozen who went out to play,
There wasn't much left at the end of the day.
For the air was so warm and the sun was so blazing
That the quick liquefaction was truly amazing.
I saw that brave party all glorious at morn,
I saw them at eve, and behold they were 'gorn'!
What fate had o'ertaken them didn't transpire,
But the reservoir level was palpably higher!

Obiter Cantata

THE BANKS OF CLYDE

THE fields were green, the flowery grove
   Was decked like a young bride,
When Ronald and his sister May
Went forth to spend the sunny day
   Upon the banks of Clyde.

The lark's sweet music filled the air,
   Wild roses waved around,
The lanes with summer bloom were bright,
Like fallen stars the daisies white
   Lay twinkling on the ground.

They crossed the meadows, climbed the hill,
   And from the grassy height
Looked down upon the winding stream,
With here a shade and there a gleam,
   A rich and wondrous sight.

They saw the stately heron stand
   Tall, silent, and alone ;
They saw the thoughtless fishes play
Just where the watchful otter lay
   Upon a dripping stone.

'What flowers are those ?' cried sister May ;
   'The tall green flags between,
Blue as the bluest summer skies
And lovely as the sweet blue eyes
   Of baby Geraldine ?'

'Forget-me-nots !   How beautiful !'
   Down, down they sped along,
Where danger lurked they did not know ;
The treacherous river swirled below
   With currents swift and strong.

To a brown willow by the brink
   Young Ronald stoutly clung,
But May dashed down as in a dream,
And far into the eddying stream
   The little maid was flung.

Now Ronald, if in your young veins
  There run true British blood,
Quick ! or that little maid must be
Swept out into the surging sea
  To perish in the flood.

He did not doubt, he did not pause,
  He leaped into the tide.
A brother's love is strong to save,
With desperate arm he fought the wave
  And reached his sister's side.

He seized her by her long brown hair,
  He struggled to the shore ;
The slippery bank at last they gain,
And in his arms o'er hill and plain
  The fainting child he bore.

Breathless, but faithful to his task,
  The distant home was won,
And she was saved.   Ah, noble boy !
Earth has no pleasure, life no joy
  Like duty bravely done.

A SUMMER CAMPAIGN

Four Botanists met on a cliff by the sea,
Old friends who had trudged over forest and lea
In search of the wonders that lurk in the bog,
Or cling to the rock and the moss-painted log.

   The hot days of August were just in their prime,
The wasps were abundant, the dust was sublime,
But the Botanists, each in his own summer rig,
Replied to dame Nature, 'We don't care a fig!
You may boil, you may roast, you may pepper or
    drown,
We're here for a week, we've escaped from the town;
We'll rifle your treasures on sandhill and fen,
We'll find out your secrets, the Where and the
    When,
But the How and the Why we acknowledge are
    harder—
One may dine at an inn, but not pry in the larder!

40

The rare, long-leaved Sundew we'll hunt on the
    moor,
And *Statice caspia* down by the shore,
Where the shrubby *S" œda* just fringes the land,
And *Salsola* spreads out his thorns on the sand.
We're in for real work, not a mere boyish game,
So kindly prepare us a welcome, old Dame.'

  And Nature looked out from her great shining
    eye,
She dried up the fens and she polished the sky ;
She soothed the sea-wind to a sweet-tempered
    breeze,
That refreshed the white sand-plains and fanned
    the hot trees ;
She opened the doors of her treasure-house wide,
From her well-beloved sons she had nothing to
    hide.
'Come, search me, and count me, and read me !'
    she said,
' I'm a riddle profound that has never been read.
You that love me, unravel the threads of my life,
So blended in beauty, so knotted with strife.
See ! I give you *carte blanche*, use my tools or my toys,
They are all at your service ; go at it, my boys !'

Then the Botanists laid down their plans for each
  day,
And carried them out in a businesslike way.
From Bawsey and Roydon and Dersingham fen
To   Heacham,   Holme,   Ringstead,   and   Huns'ton
  again,
They ransacked the land and they searched by the
  sea,
And brought back their vasculums filled with
  débris :
Rhynchospora alba and *Myrica gale*,
And *Triticum repens*, the blue *littorale*,
With *Psamma, Cakile,* and *Glaucium* and *Phleum*,
So mixed and so many, the eyes that would see
  'em
Had need to be sharp with the practice of years ;
But a Botanist's eyes are in league with his ears,
He knows by the rustle, the crunch and the crack,
One-half of the species that lie in his track.
  Lactuca virosa they found on the sand,
And a rare little Bladderwort further inland.
There were regions where *Sphagnum* and *Drosera*
  spread
Like a rich Turkey carpet in yellow and red ;

There were fens full of Cranberry, Sea-rush and
Reeds,
Where the Snipe makes his home and the Bittern
still breeds,
Where the Blackcock was flushed and the Sand-
piper ran,
And the brown Adder watched to make war upon
man,
And the Lizard slid nimbly through heather and
fern,
Or lay like a stick by the slow-gliding burn;
Where *Helix virgata* half covered the grass,
As the pale, rayless *Aster* the muddy morass;
Where *Osmunda* sat throned in a leaf-sheltered
nook,
And the slender *Œnanthe* peered up from the
brook.
Salicornia, Narthecium, Pinguicula, most
Of the life that is anywhere seen on the coast
Or the heaths or the bogs of old England was
there,
And the Botanists found it, and touched it with care.
Not theirs the rude culture that grabs at all cost
E'en the last fading relics of forms nearly lost;

True lovers of Nature, they would not destroy
The wild beauties she nursed with such pride and
such joy.
So the hours and the days sped away on swift
wings,
And the end came at last, as to all pleasant things ;
And the Botanists parted, each went on his way :
If such meeting were ever again, who could say ?
The chances of life were against it, they knew,
But their hearts were at one and their friendship
was true.
And in life or in death they all swore by St.
Dunstan,
They'd remember those days round the red cliffs of
Huns'ton.

THE SHADOW OF BEAUTY

CHEERLY, old comrades, cheerly
  Spins the wild world on its way,
And the woods are as green as ever
  Though we grow old and grey.

The universe laughs to the Ages
  At the wonderful whirligig game,
The bubbling of souls to the surface
  While the Great Soul is ever the same.

And the Ages laugh back.   They are merry,
  These always young Æons of Time,
For the game is the Riddle of Beauty,
  And the answer is—wisdom sublime!

What mean we to fret and to falter
  When all the green world is at play?
While the stars sing their carols around us
  In the joy of perpetual day?

If we were as wise and as ancient,
  We too should sing pæans of praise
For life, with its glory and gladness,
  In the arms of the Ancient of Days.

But we lie like young babes in our cradle,
  On the verge of the measureless night,
And the roses that cling round the window
  Mix their shade with the morning light.

We shall know in the strength of our manhood,
  As we gaze on the broad sky above,
That it is but the shadow of Beauty
  Which chequers the sunlight of Love.

THE PEDLAR'S WIFE

If I had a crown of gold,
   And a palace like the Queen's,
And every day the cash to pay
   For a dinner of bacon and greens;
   I would not change—not I—
   My wandering pedlar life,
And the love of my own sweet Marjorie,
   My bonny little Highland wife!

Shall I tell you how I found
   This jewel bright and rare ?—
I was out for a spree, in the north countrie,
   On the morning of Edinburgh Fair.
   In those wild young days a Fair
   Seemed the jolliest thing in life—
Till I met my own sweet Marjorie,
   My bonny little Highland wife!

I was up with the sun that morning,
　　When a letter came, to say
My old mother lay dead in Leicestershire,
　　Three hundred miles away.
　　I thought a big black cloud
　　Had dropt down over the sun,
For all the light went out like night,
　　And I knew my day was done.

　　The dear old mother dead,
　　And I so far away!
O the grief and the pain!　I feel them again
　　As they tortured me all that day.
　　But a lassie came by in the gloamin'—
　　Came merrily tripping on—
And she spoke to me—sweet Marjorie!
　　She said, 'What ails thee, mon?'

　　'Twas only a little word,
　　And a look from a kind blue eye,
But it touched a soft part in my troubled heart
　　And it made me sob and cry.

Then Marjorie, dear little birdie !
She pitied my lonely grief:
And a woman's pity, in man's distress,
    Is sure and sweet relief.

I looked in her loving eyes,
Her gentle voice I heard ;
' My lad,' she said, ' she isna dead !'
    But I answered never a word.
    ' She isna dead, but sleepeth !
What gars ye dole and greet?
It 's na sae lang till the trumpets clang,
    And the mither and bairn shall meet !'

What may not a woman's voice
For the children of sorrow do,
When the warm words start from a noble heart
    And a spirit brave and true ?
    I know what it did for me—
    It opened the heavenly gates,
And I saw the bright land where the angels
        stand,
    And the dear old mother waits !

My blessing upon thee, Marjorie!
A poor man's wife art thou.
But if I loved thee well that day,
I love thee better now!
For the same pure faithful heart,
And the same persuading voice,
Have banished tears these twenty years,
And made my days rejoice.

Oh, if I had a crown of gold,
And a palace like the Queen's,
And every day the cash to pay
For a dinner of bacon and greens;
I would not change—not I—
My wandering pedlar life,
And the love of my own sweet Marjorie,
My bonny little Highland wife!

ASPIRATION

HIGHER and higher
Leaps up the golden fire,
Beyond the sky, beyond the flaming stars,
Beyond the boundaries of eternal night.

Higher, still higher,
Shall the strong soul aspire,
Through all the encumbering mists of ignorance,
Into the heaven of wisdom, love, and light.

Higher, yet higher!
Pause not, young soul, nor tire.
The way is toilsome, but the prize is large—
The power of Knowledge and the joy of Right.

IRENE

Ye dancing waves of ocean,
  Ye birds that float in air,
Tinting the sun-white landscape
  With motion soft and rare,
Ye touch my heart with a memory sweet
  Of a face that is far away—
A face that I love and a form that is dear,
  My child who is twelve to-day.

For she is a sun-white spirit,
  Pure as the morning dew,
Strong with the strength of an upright soul,
  Stately and calm and true ;
And if ever a shade of the world's unrest
  Shall darken her pathway bright,
The angels of God shall guide her feet
  Back to the bowers of light.

BACCHUS THE WINE-BIBBER

BACCHUS the wine-bibber,
  When he was slandered,
Shook his green ivy-wreath,
  Waved his red standard.

'Down!' sang his manly voice,
  'Down with the traitor
Whose babbling tongue belies
  Great Mother Nature!

'She knows the needs of man
  Long ago taught her;
None lives by bread alone
  Nor bread and water.

'Drink! and live manly lives,
  Faithful to duty,
Bright with good fellowship,
  Rounded with beauty.

' Curse not what Providence
   Wisely provided,
Wine, that should join the hands
   Which strife divided.

' Wine for the solace of
   Souls that are weary ;
Wine for the winter night
   Snow-bound and eerie.

' Bread for the homely life,
   Meat for the darer ;
Wine for the crown of all,
   Subtlest food-bearer.

' Spirit of energy,
   Brain and nerve feeder,
In the heart's deep despair
   Blest interceder !

' Thee shall the wise man use
   And not defile thee,
Thee shall the good defend
   When fools revile thee ! '

ODE FOR THE CHICAGO EXHIBITION

1892

ALL that is boldest, and all that is loveliest,
  Worship of Art, and rebellion of Soul!
Spirits that spurn the rude bonds of convention,
  Bound for the Best, while the centuries roll.

  Spread the broad banner!
  The world-welcome banner!
  Here, in Chicago, proud Queen of the Age!

Peace to all lands! 'Tis the day of Humanity.
  Fling wide the gates, we are brothers all
    round!—
Northman and Southernman, Gaul, Greek, and
    Teuton,
  Room for the nations on Liberty's ground!

What mean those monster guns, blazing and
  thunderous ?
Why swarms the sea with the hellhounds of war?
Lift the great anthem of ' Freedom and Fellowship,'
  Christian and Moslem, Cross, Crescent and Star !

Not with the rage of defiance and bitterness
  Meet we to-day, to make history dark.
Glad shall our children be, glad that their fathers
  Strove for the highest, like the heaven-soaring
  lark.

Let this World's Fair be for aid, not for victory.
  Brothers we stand in its sun-lighted hall,
Raising one song to the God of the Nations,
  Changeless and boundless, great Father of all !

Spread the broad banner !
The world-welcome banner !
Here, in Chicago, proud Queen of the Age !

A SONG

I

Sing me a song of the waning day
   In the rich midsummer's prime,
With the blackbird piping his mellow lay
   To the far-off curfew chime.
Sing, O sing to my longing soul!
For the joys that we loved when life was young
     and full
       Return no more!

II

Tell me a tale of a weeping maid
   In a castle by the sea,
Of a broken heart and a love betrayed,
   And a dream that may not be.
Sing, O sing, for my soul is sad
With the weight of a life that was once so young
     and glad,
       Now worn and sore!

III

Chant me the psalm of a warrior strong
  In the storm of the battle's press,
A psalm of victory, loud and long,
  High o'er the strain and the stress.
Sing, O sing, for my soul aspires
To the heavenly hills and the song that never
    tires.
      The fight is o'er !

SPRING AND SUMMER

SPRING in the fields and the garden,
   Spring on the sunny hills,
And a joy that cannot be spoken
   Runs in the dancing rills.

See, here are the daisies, my Jenny,
   And here are the harebells blue;
And oh, but I love you, Jenny,
   Little wife so trusty and true!

Yes, let him roll and be happy
   His merry eyes sing like a bird,
For baby was born in the springtime,
   And his wakening soul is stirred—

Stirred with a music we hear not,
   A far-off sound of delight,
From wings that are softly unfolding
   And buds that are bursting to light.

Spring for the children, my Jenny,
   But summer for me and for you !
Those hours of fickle beauty,
   Thank God, we have long passed through.

Summer with song and with sunshine,
   And love that has learnt to be true ;
And the joy of the world to me, Jenny,
   Is to live in its light with you.

For the richness, the fulness, the splendour,
   Of the love of a husband and wife,—
This is the best of it all, Jenny,
   The crown of the wave of life !

OUR COTTAGE

Clematis, ivy, and eglantine,
   Roses purple and white,
Starry jasmine and creeping vine
Garnish a sweet little home of mine
   With fragrance and beauty and light.

Flowers without and flowers within,
   But I stand at the garden gate
Heedless of roses or clematis sweet,
For there in the doorway are two little feet,
   And only for me they wait.

Two eyes like pools in a fairy dell,
   Two lips like the gates of heaven—
Those coral gates that stand apart,
With, just for the hungry and longing heart,
   A glimpse of the angels given.

Two arms outstretched with a yearning grace
    Like the young moon in the west,
Two hearts made one in the beauty of love !
With a joy that is registered somewhere above
    I clasp my prize to my breast.

Ah, beautiful home !   In the visions of morn
    You rise like a sunny dream,
A flowery isle on the river of life,
And I in the arms of my fairy wife
    Float down with the singing stream.

LOVE'S ANTICIPATION

It is a cold March morning
  With a sharp and piercing breeze,
The frost lies on the meadows
  And tips the ghostly trees.

The low sunbeams faintly sloping
  From a sky of pale sea-blue,
Are changed to icy spangles
  As they touch the frozen dew.

There are lines of burnished lances
  In the fields of springing corn,
And on long sprays in the hedges
  There are silver banners borne ;

But the fairy hosts are sleeping,
  Their glittering arms are piled,
Not yet the morning herald
  Winds his sky-horn clear and wild.

In the air is no bird-music,
  No voice nor sound below;
I seem to hear the Hours
  In their long march pacing slow.

And from the cold broad heavens
  Like a dial-plate outspread,
I see Time's shadow sweeping
  The records of the dead.

So still it is and lonely,
  So spirit-like and keen,
I gaze upon the face of God
  With only death between.

And the dark gulf seems narrowed
  To a strip of ice-bound sea.
Launch out, my soul, and anchor
  In those regions of the free!

Ah! what glory streams around me!
  Not of eye, and not of ear.
Spirit-splendours, mind-illuming,
  Are the light and music here.

Sphæral songs through ages swelling
  Noon upon Arabian plains,
Are but shadows of the beauty
  That my raptured soul sustains.

No horizon, space-surrounded,
  Drops its veil before my gaze,
Here the Hours march no longer
  Through the circles of the days.

Floating on a sea of gladness,
  All my spirit seems to move
In the ever waveless current
  Of the universal Love.

Not alone; the heavenly mansions
  Shine not for a favoured few:
No! the Father gifts His children
  With the holy, pure, and true.

E

Clouds of passion may defile it,
　　Earthborn vapours quench the flame,
Yet there is a Love that fails not,
　　What He gave He will reclaim.

Here the myriad throngs of being
　　Lifted from their lower spheres,
Wreathe around me, love-entwining,
　　Breathing love into my ears.

Ah ! the shell of self falls from me
　　And the God-like life begins ;
Goal long sought, whose crown of blessing
　　Only Love the victor wins.

Glowing thoughts and large affections
　　Like spring-fountains fill my soul,
And a boundless love embracing
　　As one brother-heart the whole.

Wells where happiness lay hidden
　　Now o'erflow their crystal brims ;
In the level flood of kindness
　　Evenly my spirit swims.

Gliding onward, not unguided;
   Loving all, but seeking One,
As the flower that lights the landscape
   Turns for ever to the sun.

Sympathies remain in heaven,
   Change not with the changing state;
True as the returning comet
   Flies the spirit to its mate.

Doctrines of absorbing essence,
   Love rejects and reason spurns;
I and Thou shall be eternal
   While the lamp of being burns.

Wandering through these realms of beauty
   Steeped in gladness, still I seek
For that One whose spirit only
   To my heart of hearts can speak.

Come, dear angel! fill this longing,
   Restless soul that yearns to be
Mingling from its deepest fountains
   Thought and sympathy with thee.

Through the swelling choir of heaven
 Steals a soft voice to my ear,
An answering tone—the soul I sought,
 Ah! boundless, endless joy, 'tis here!

.   .   .   .   .

The vision passes. Gales of winter
 Sweep along the freezing plain;
But the March wind, keen and piercing,
 Cannot chill my breast again.

A PANTOUM

O Sun with the golden pinions !
  O Moon with the silver veil !
Deep in yon star-dominions
  Ye spread the filmy sail.

O Moon with the silver veil,
  Planets that wander wide,
Ye spread the filmy sail
  Over night's purple tide !

Planets that wander wide,
  What seek ye in the deep?
Over night's purple tide
  Ye sing though the whirlwind sleep.

What seek ye in the deep?
   Silence and night are there.
Ye sing though the whirlwind sleep
   Praise to the Good and Fair!

Silence and night are there
   Deep in yon star-dominions.
Praise to the Good and Fair,
   O Sun with the golden pinions!

DOUBT

FATHER ! in life's shadowy passes
　Cold and stern and drear,
Where black crags and withered grasses
　Chill the soul with fear;

Where no sunbeam lights the distance,
　And no wayside flower
Lifts the burden of existence
　For one hopeful hour;

'Tis then our wavering trust is tried,
　The lamp of faith burns low,
Life seems so dark, the world so wide,
　Time's loitering feet so slow!

CHANGE

Life has its shadows, dim and danger-fraught,
   Its midnight paths where all is black and blind,
And terror-stricken souls tread tremblingly,
   Horrors in front and beggared hopes behind.

Life has its summer days serene and bright,
   When the still leaves lie dreaming in the noon,
And happy toilers wipe their ringing scythes
   In the cool eve beneath the fragrant moon.

Life has its Spring and Autumn; the round globe
   Is rich with changeful hues, and though the boy
Climbs to the man through storms and tears, his
      heart
   Thrills with the music of an untold joy.

HARMONIC

She looked upon the world, and knew its need;
She saw the love that burned about its heart,
And the great burden of darkness that entombed
The living beauty, and her strong soul rose
Like an archangel.—' World!' she cried, ' awake!'
And laid her light hand with electric touch
Upon the darkness, till the white beam sprang,
And all the buried love leaped up and smiled.

Only a woman, yet the universe
Answered with subtle sympathy, like harps
That sing because the rippling wind goes by.

DESPAIR

When the storm gathers on the slumbering sea,
And the white-crested warriors, rank by rank,
Leap from their ambush at the thunder's call,
And, like a mountain torrent wild with rage,
Crash on their victim—what shall man avail
With all his majesty of steel and steam
To ward the onslaught?   Gulfed and torn and
    battered,
The proud ship shrinks into an ocean toy!

On such a treacherous and unsteady world
Humanity is launched to fight and die!
At night the restful silence, but at morn
The roar, the rage, the rasping torture of life!
The fears that drown the sunshine, the wild horrors
Wherein the blue gleam of a distant hope
Grows livid and cankerous, and the gates of hell
Seem the last refuge of the hunted soul!

STEP BY STEP

STEP by step the climber rises,
  Step by step our goal we reach ;
Not all to-day,
  But winning what we may,
Keep we brave hearts, and eyes that see afar
That glorious day, crowned with the morning
    star,
Which all earth's heroes claim, and all her
    prophets preach.

OUR JUNE BABY

BEAUTIFUL Soul, leaping out from the dark,
  With eyes of the midsummer blue,
White roses are blooming, the winds are awake,
Bird-music is ringing from bower and brake,
  All the world has a welcome for you!

So calm and so silent, so soft and so fair,
  Just sipping the sweetness of Earth!
When the white rose is dead, and the winds are
      at rest,
What wonder-lit vision shall live in your breast
  Of the flowers that encircled your birth?

The pathways of life may be shadowed by storm,
  The heart may be weeping with care,
But under the shadow a rose-tinted gleam
From the light of lost memories shall flash like a
      dream
  And sweeten the storm-tainted air.

70

The river that creeps through the sands to the
   sea
  Was born where the cataracts rage,
In the home of the winds on some far-away hill,
And the freshness of mountain air clings to it
   still,
  In the noiseless repose of its age.

So the sound of bird-music in dreams of the past
  Shall keep your heart tender and kind,
And the scent of June roses shall float round
   your bed
When the years have dropped snow on our little
   one's head,
  And the joy of the world lies behind.

HOME

Home! though we left it in grief and in heart-
  sickness;
  Home! though its peace has been clouded with
  pain,—
All that the wide world can give to the wanderer
  Lures the true heart from its hearthstone in
  vain.

Here gleamed the sun on our earliest victories,
  Here bloomed the flower of our love in its pride;
Here are the friends who have stood by us faith-
  fully,
  Here lie the dead who have fall'n at our side.

Once more we tread the dear soil of our fatherland!
  Tide-waves of memory rush thick with their foam.
Hail to the friends who have never forgotten us!
  Hail to the voices that welcome us home!

HYMN FOR THE AGED

FATHER, Thou hast led my feet
   Far along life's varied way,
To this bower of calm retreat
   Where I rest in peace to-day,
While silver hair and failing breath
Warn me of approaching death.

In my childhood long ago
   I could feel my Father's hand,
And I will not let it go
   Now that on life's verge I stand.
O my Father, Guide, and Friend,
All my soul to Thee I bend!

Over many a rugged way
   In the gloom of grief and pain,

79

When it seemed the clouded day
    Never could be bright again,
I have seen the sun arise
And fill with tears my thankful eyes.

    Standing by the open grave
        Of many a loved one gone before,
    The young, the beautiful, the brave,
        Whose love would sweeten life no more,
I have heard my Father say,
'Trust them to My care to-day.'

    In sunny hours of love and light,
        Through years that passed like happy dreams,
    In the shade of wintry night,
        Or basking in the summer beams,—
Always, and in every place,
I have seen my Father's face.

    Now the lengthening shadows run
        Down life's pathway far behind,
And the broad red western sun
        Smiles upon me calm and kind.
'Come!' he says, 'the hour is near,
The day is past, sweet night is here.'

Yes, sweet night! my Father dear,
    When I close my eyes in sleep
At Thy call, I shall not fear
    To pass into the unknown deep,
Leaning all my soul on Thee,
Trusting where I cannot see.

LOVE

KNOWING that poison
　Was mixed in the bowl,
He seized the gold goblet
　And quaffed down the whole.
'Fool!' say'st thou?　Be silent!
　The strong-handed soul
Shall mount the fierce lightning
　And flash to its goal.

Harmless the poison-cup,
　Tempests obey,
When Love takes the rudder
　And fronts the red day.
Love the bold hero
　Who dares to be gay
While the flushed coward Passion
　Turns trembling away.

THE MUSIC OF LIFE

The morning song that the stars sang together
Soft in the summer daybreak, and the light
That gleamed along the dewy vales of youth :—
    How pure!   How tender!   How divinely sweet!

The rich rose-lighted midsummer of life,
When all the garden paths were warm and fragrant,
And the soul leaped with masterful delight :—
    How strong!   How hopeful!   How divinely proud!

The sumptuous Eve that in the porch of death
Stood undismayed, with gold and purple veiling
The gathered splendour of life's ripening thought :—
    How rich !   How lustrous !   How divinely great !

The white-robed winter toiling in the silence
Unseen, unknown, a centre-work of love
That the grave hides not from the heart of God :—
    How still !   How perfect !   How divinely calm !

Memorials

WILLIAM NAPIER REEVE

ÆT. 76

FAREWELL, old friend !
Once more we greet thee ! not as at the end
Of life, or love, or friendship, but as one
Passed from our dreamland to the morning sun.
  Farewell, old friend !
They who have loved thee long,
Known the brave spirit and the generous heart,
  And seen the ranks of wrong
Before thy vigorous arm break and depart,
   They shall keep green thy name
    While centuries roll,
And write upon the pillared porch of Fame,
   ' Peace to a noble soul ! '

1888.

GEORGE BARTON FRANKLIN

ÆT. 78

Our gentle scholar!   Resolute as man,
Tender as woman.   In an aimless world
He stood for virtue, purity, and truth,
Bating no jot though rabid scorn should rage.
    He climbed with us the alpine road of life,
Cheery and calm even to the serried edge
Of the last pass, and waving faint adieus
Scaled the dark ridge and reached the promised
        land.
    Henceforth the star-set dome of memory
Gleams with an added jewel.   Let the grave
Welcome its own, coffined with tears of love,
And shrouded in the mysteries of death.
For us there is no death, no loss, no woe!
God's beauty gilds the universe with joy,
Tears have no entrance where the soul has vision.

    1893.

JAMES PLANT, F.G.S.

ÆT. 74

ONE of our pioneers, one of our leaders,
 Gone to his rest in the grave !
  Lay him down tenderly
  Think of him cheerily—
 He was so bright, and so brave !

Never a crag on the hills of old Charnwood,
 Never a rock on the plain,
  But rang to his hammer—
  Alas, the sweet clamour
 That never may ring there again !

Gone, with the store of his long-garnered wisdom ;
 Gone from his boulders and blocks !
  Bronzed with wild weather,
  Like winter-blown heather,
 Aud sprinkled with snow on his locks.

Oft in the forest, the vale, or the quarry,
  Haunts of the snake and the bird,
    Under the blaze
    Of the old summer days,
  How have we hung on his word!

How has he pictured pre-adamite turmoils,
  When mountain on mountain was hurled
    By forces volcanic,
    Earth-shattering, Titanic,
  That built up the bones of this world!

All the dark puzzles, the unanswered questions
  Which Science strewed thick in his way,
    Will she now solve them?
    Or will Death dissolve them
  In light from the limitless day?

Wondering and doubting, we peer through the
    shadows
  That circle our playground of life,
    And hear in the distance
    Wild cries of resistance,
  The echoes of strain and of strife.

He who has forded the foam of the river
    Heeds not the roar of its tide ;
      But we who are under
      The spell of its thunder
    Still shrink on the hither side.

1892.

RICHARD WADDINGTON

ÆT. 65

Alas! for a soul that was born in the dreamland
  Of beauty and song where the amaranth blows!
In the winter of life he fell, shattered and lonely,
  The treasures he hoarded lie lost in the snows.

Bright with a happiness grief could not darken,
  Child of the Muses, immortally wise,
All that was best of him Heaven shall rekindle,
  All that was weak shall be left where he lies.

1892.

WILLIAM BARFOOT

(DIED DURING THE MAYORALTY OF HIS SON)

ÆT. 78

LET the worn pilgrim pass!
Is he not happy? what can life give more?
Has he not seen the glory of his race?
Honour hath crowned him, not on his own head,
But on his boy's.   Content, nay, glad and merry,
He shakes Death's hand—'Hail, friend! now lead
    me home!'

1876.

MRS. MARY TODD

ÆT. 68

O VENERABLE heart!
That through the paths of pain went bravely down
To meet the veiled face of the dark Unknown,
     And take with Death thy part;

Buoyed by no passionate faith,
No shallow comfort of redeeming blood,
No trust in antique creeds to bar the flood
     Of sin-avenging wrath;

But filled with living love,
And a warm joy in all things beautiful,
And in life's quiet pathway dutiful
     To wisdom from above.

Clear-eyed to winnow out
Good grain from chaff; thirsty for truths, and keen
To brush away mere words, that ' come between
    The soul and its high doubt.'

Too honest and too brave
To hide or fear whatever light can show;
Daring to trust in God, and not to know
    How He will save.

Like the fleet star
That slides along the archways of the Night,
Thou leav'st a train of memories soft and bright,
    Good deeds that shine afar.

O venerable heart!
Thy crown is won, thy battle-flag is furled.
Wake from the slumber of this twilight world
    And take with Life thy part!

1868.

ELIZABETH MARY DOBELL

ÆT. 3

LITTLE Elsie! darling Elsie!
  What has stayed your restless feet?
What has quenched the living love-light
  In your eyes so blue and sweet?

Merry as a lark this morning,
  Brave and shining like the sun!—
When he shines again to-morrow,
  Will he miss you, little one?

He has other eyes to shine on,
  Other heads to touch with gold—
What have we like laughing Elsie?
  Pet lamb of our little fold!

O great Death! be gentle with her!
  Lead her to some happy spot!
Who will tend our helpless darling
  In a home where we are not?

Surely God must love His children,
  If they love their own so well,—
Ah, then He will love our Elsie,
  How much more than we can tell!

We will trust Him with our treasure;
  Trust Him always—at all cost!
Though our hearts are pierced with sorrow,
  Elsie, dear, you are not lost!

In the mansions of our Father,
  With the children of all time,
Nurtured in the heavenly wisdom,
  You shall grow into your prime.

And when all the years are over,
  The dark years which look so long,
O the joy to clasp our Elsie,
  Grown to ripeness fair and strong!

G

Lord, if yet we cannot thank Thee
　　For Thy gifts of death and pain,
Still we trust that through Thy goodness,
　　Present loss is final gain.

So we take our daily duties
　　Firmly, if with tearful eyes;
Bringing strength, and hope, and patience,
　　From the grave where Elsie lies.

1867.

FLORENCE JANE DOBELL

ÆT. 21

THOSE helpful hands, those ready feet,
   That never went astray,
The loving heart, the smiling eyes,
   All dead and passed away !

Dear, faithful Florrie ! not in vain
   Your generous soul was spent,
For others' hopes and others' joys
   On kindly cares intent.

What fruit one little flower may bear
   In God's world, who shall say ?
The beauty of a stainless life
   No grave can hide away.

Go to your rest, white flower of earth,
    Beneath the winter snow ;
Only in springtime or in heaven
    Such tender buds may blow.

1876.

MRS. JOSEPH WHETSTONE

WIDOW, ÆT. 76

A TENDER woman's heart, faithful and fond,
Left, like a desolate and lonely wreck,
Upon life's outmost shore !
           The Rescue Ship,
Death's lifeboat, manned with messengers of hope,
Flies to the signal of distress : the wreck
Is lifted, floated, all her broken cords
And torn white sails made beautiful once more !
And soft winds lead her forth caressingly
From that dark strand into a summer sea.

MARIANNE CHAPMAN

ÆT. 76

PASSED, like a breath of the summer air,
  Fresh and sweet and bright!
A soul that was strong and a form that was fair
  In the long-ago morning light.

My childhood's friend! There are sixty years
  Between the then and now,
But I see you still with the rich brown curls
  Circling the rounded brow.

Life was no drowsy game to you,
  Love and labour and thought
For the joy of God's little ones hallowed the years
  And the soulful days they brought.

Shall not the spirit that toiled so well
   Toil on, with the grave between?
The Eternal Good that shall always be
   Wastes not the good that has been.

W. E. GLADSTONE

ÆT. 88

O ENGLAND ! guarded well
    Round all thy valorous coasts,
By signal-light and swinging bell,
    And tramp of watchful hosts.
There is one light burned out,
The loftiest light that lit the whole broad land
From western crags to eastern slopes, and held
    The world in wonder.
Let the flags droop, and let the trumpets wail,
Our best is gone !   Closed is the wondrous tale !
Yet the long line of Heroes shall not fail.

    Proud England ! proud no more,
      Humbled with sudden loss
    Of this great, saintly warrior,
      This Hero of the Cross.

The lamp he set so high,
The sacred lamp of honour, truth, and right,
Let it burn on with clear white flame, as though
    His hand still held it.
Well may the flags droop and the trumpets wail,
Our best is gone, closed is the wondrous tale ;
Yet England's line of Heroes must not fail !

    Great England ! strong to wield
      The sceptre of the sea ;
    To bear abroad o'er flood and field
      The banner of the free,
    Hark to that solemn bell !
The warning voice of angels in the air :
' Now, England, now is Fate beside thee, now
    Thine hour of peril !
Let the flags droop, and let the trumpets wail,
Thy best is gone ; closed is that wondrous tale.
Pray God thy line of Heroes do not fail ! '

May 19, 1898.

Anniversaries

With the first smile of the Spring
   Comes our little Ida's birthday,
Whispering of the swallow's wing,
   Laughing as the merry earth may;
      For the snowdrop's bell is swinging,
      And the leafless elms are ringing
         With the thrice-cock's roundelay.

Little daughter pale and slim,
   Life is opening fast before you,
And the lighted mists grow dim
   That in childhood floated o'er you.
      Hearest thou life's rushing river?
      Fear not, the eternal Giver
         Of all life and love is near you.

February 23, 1887.

I THANK the universal Lord of life,
    That to my care was given
A soul so fair to be my earthly wife,
    My spirit-friend in heaven.

I know not how she should have cared to give
    Her sweet young lips to me,
But in the midst of miracles we live,
    Each breath a mystery.

And in the strange complexities of life
    There is a faultless Guide :
The trusting soul shall find His miracles
    Are richly justified.

September 19, 1892.

STATELY as the pine-tree,
    Fearless and serene,
    Climbing ever upward
    Like the ivy green ;
Fronting on the mountain-track the high untrodden
    snows,
On her brow the star of hope, and in her hand the
    rose,
    The deep-eyed maiden goes.

    In the far dim distance
    When the years are fled,
    Up among the crown of crags
    On the mountain's head,
Where her feet may climb no further toward the
    starry skies,
God's light upon her snow-touched brow and in her
    closing eyes,
    The deep-eyed maiden lies.

June 19, 1897.

Life like a gathering river runs
  Between the banks of Time,
A tiny moss-bed at its source,
  In front, God's heaven sublime.

The morning dew upon the moss
  Delights our infant eyes,
Till the great thoughts with gathering years
  Rush forward to the skies.

For us, dear love, the mossy fount
  Fades in the distance blue,
But all God's palaces of light
  Are bursting into view.

May 29, 1890.

OLD friendships, like old heirlooms, may lie hid
In musk and lavender, and gather grace
And reverence and the sanctity of age,
Yet perish not, nor lose their mellowed beauty.
    And on life's festal days we lift with care
The rich and delicate memories of the past
And wear them on our hearts, and let them lie
And gleam in the old sunlight, while our thoughts
Ascend in prayers of thankfulness.   Old friends
Are like rare jewels in an antique ring
That with long shining side by side have learnt
To sparkle in tune, and make a harmony
Of their mixed beams.   So hearts that once have
        beat
In unison, though years and continents
Divide them, feel the sympathetic chord
Struck in the long ago, and for a moment,
As the wave wandering through the plains of space
Rolls by, ring out together with answering tones.

December 4, 1893.

H

A MICHAELMAS Daisy fair to see,
Grew in my garden and smiled at me.
I kissed it, and loved it, and heard it say,
'I shall get grown up, I suppose, some day.
Then I shall work for the world and you,
But what can an eight-years-old daisy do?'
And a voice in her heart said : ' Do the right!
Learn all day, and be thankful at night !'

November 2, 1890.

LIFT up your eyes, young aspirant ! the day
Is breaking, and the sounds of life and labour
Summon the sleeper from his boyish dreams.
　Who would lie dozing when the lark is up,
The blackbird piping, and the happy wren
Cheering with jubilant song his busy mate?
　A child no more !　Gird on the arms of man-
　　hood !
There are great deeds to do ere daylight fail,
Battles to fight, and victories to win !
And every faithful heart that will not quail,
And every vigorous arm that wearies not
To do God's work, shall learn the unspeakable
　　joy
Of glorious labour for the sacred Right.

April 10, 1891.

MERRY gleam of autumn sunshine,
  Rippling rivulet!
Midst the dead leaves of November
  Like a living rosebud set!

Happy be the years that face you!
  Yet, not only so—
Grief must grind what joy shall polish
  That the soul may nobly grow,—

Like a gem that has no beauty
  Till the ruthless wheel
Rasps it into glittering facets
  That its glowing heart reveal.

And beneath those dancing ringlets,
  And within those loving eyes,
God has put a soul, my darling!
  Make it beautiful and wise.

November 2, 1894.

Ten thousand souls on this fortunate day
  Out from the darkness sprang;
The sweetest and purest went floating away
Seeking some nest where its flight should stay,
And soft in the beams of a morning in May
On the soul of its fellow that sweet soul lay,
  And two souls with music rang.

September 19, 1852—*May* 29, 1877.

WITH an old friend's best wishes, that though Fate
Has fixed his birthday on an awkward date,
Jumping from twenty-four to twenty-eight,
By leaps as long he may grow wise and great,
Or learn this simple truth, at any rate,
That what falls rarely falls with greater weight,
And that even birthdays may be better late
Than never !

February 29, 1852.

www.ingramcontent.com/pod-product-compliance
Lightning Source LLC
Chambersburg PA
CBHW020754020726
47495CB00008B/2423